A Children's Book About

BEING BOSSY

Managing Editor: Ellen Klarberg
Copy Editor: Annette Gooch
Editorial Assistant: Lana Eberhard
Art Director: Jennifer Wiezel
Production Artist: Gail Miller
Illustration Designer: Bartholomew
Inking Artist: Berenice Happé Iriks
Coloring Artist: Berenice Happé Iriks
Lettering Artist: Linda Hanney
Typographer: Communication Graphics

A Children's Book About

BEING BOSSY

By Joy Berry

GROLIER ENTERPRISES CORP.

This book is about Katie and her friend Tami.

Reading about Katie and Tami can help you understand and deal with **being bossy**.

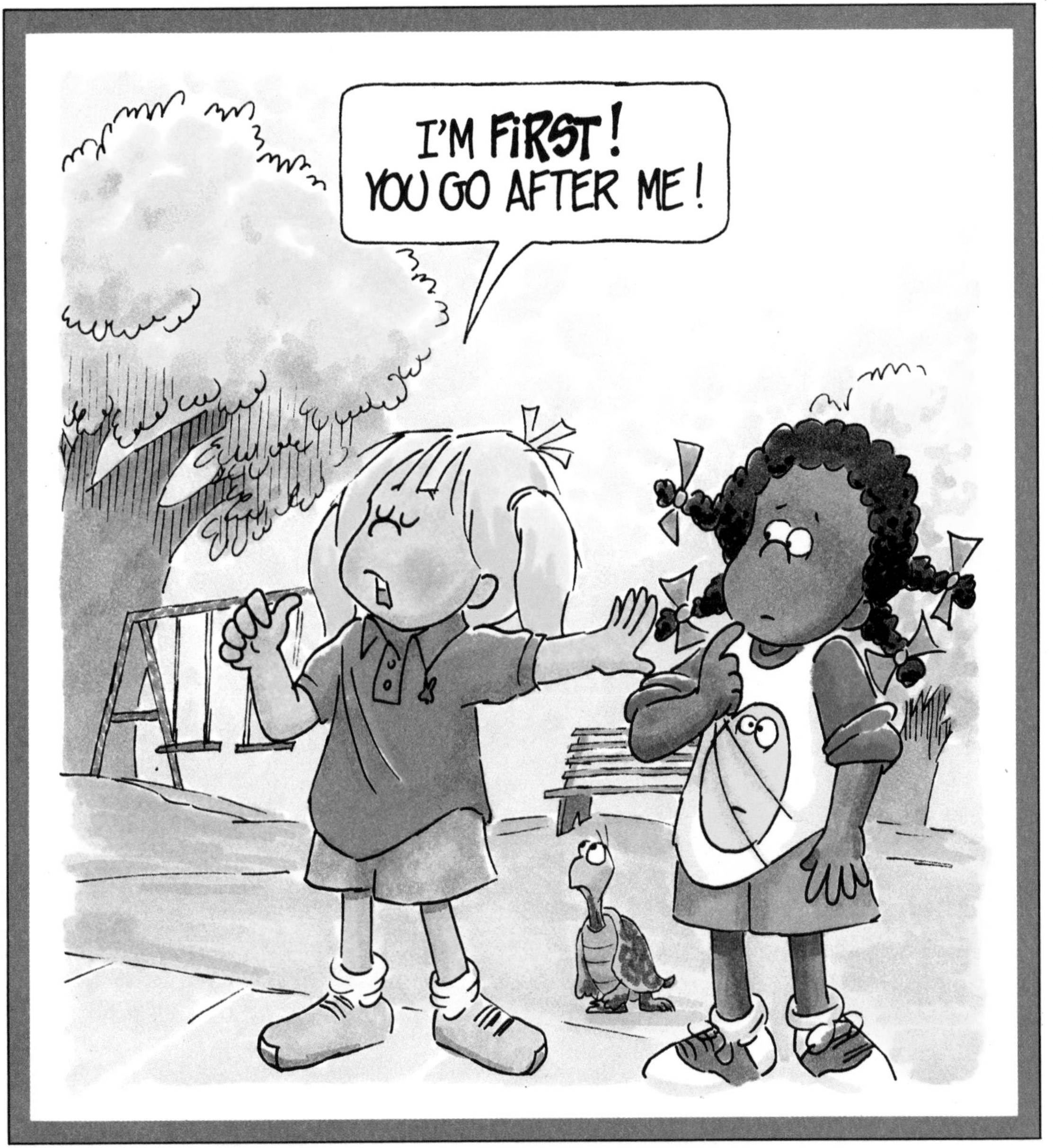
I'M FIRST! YOU GO AFTER ME!

Bossy people want to have their way all the time.

Bossy people think they know what is best for everyone. They think they know what everyone should do.

Bossy people like to tell others what to do.
They expect others to obey them.

Sometimes bossy people try to *bribe others.*

They promise things to get people to obey them.

Sometimes bossy people try to *threaten others.*

They say they will go away or not play if people do not obey them.

Sometimes bossy people try to *frighten others.*

They act as though they might hurt the people who do not obey them.

Most people want to have their own way some of the time.

They do not want others always telling them what to do. They do not like to be bossed.

If you are like most people, you do not want to be bossed. It is important to treat other people the way you want to be treated.

If you do not like being bossed, you must not be bossy.

AREN'T YOU GOING TO PLAY WITH ME?
NO! YOU'RE TOO BOSSY!
THAT GOES FOR ME TOO!

Try not to be bossy. Remember that it is not fair for you to have your way all the time.

Take turns choosing what to do when you are with someone else. Let the other person choose one activity, and you choose the next.

Select an acceptable activity when it is your turn to choose. The activity should be:

- safe,
- something your parents allow you to do, and
- something that everyone can enjoy.

Be a good sport when others have their turn to choose an activity. Do what they choose if the activity is safe and something your parents allow you to do.

Try not to complain when others choose an activity. Do whatever you can to make the activity enjoyable for everyone.

Try not to be bossy. Do not bribe, threaten, or frighten anyone into obeying you.

No one likes to be bossed. If you do not
want to be bossed, you must not be bossy.